PEACE IN NO PEACE

IFE ADENIRAN

Table of Contents

DEDICATION

I dedicate this book to my parents, for their love and support.

Also, to Da Eagles' World int'l, the organization that groomed me.

Above all, to El-Shaddai, God almighty, who has made all things well.

PROLOGUE.

March 22, this day, this particular day is one important day that will linger on her mind for a very long time. It will play hide and seek in a corner of her heart and will refuse to depart.

She looks at her mother's body being wheeled away, covered in white cloth, creating a tent on that bed. She releases her breath; a breath she never knows she is holding and turns away as her brothers place their hands on both sides of her shoulders. Their eyes are also as clammy as a windscreen in the rain and as red as palm oil, occasioned by the cascade of tears that have generously streamed from them.

Mayowa and Muyiwa shake their heads sideways as their eyes linger on the wheeled bed dissolving out of their sight. Nothing else could exist before them, it all blurs away like a dream, wafting away like a wind.

Cynthia kicks away the last comer, the last droplet of tear that is dropping off her face. It's enough. She's had enough.

Chapter 1: THE PARTY MEETING

Cynthia looks from left to right, then jumps. She takes in a deep breath and smiles after she lands, realizing no one caught her.

'Lucky me,' she heaves.

Cynthia nurses a burning love for parties, she cares less about books, businesses and any other things her dad wants for her. In her supposed smartness, she always finds a way to sneak out and party, something she can spend her whole doing.

She's slender and brown-skinned with long fingers and nails which she mostly paints nude or white. Full dark hair and cream-coloured teeth, even after using several teeth-whitening products. She's a college student in her final year but never in any class nor even in school as a whole. She knows her way around to never get a carry-over.

Cynthia adjusts her backpack and treks a short distance to meet the uber she has already ordered.

‘Let's go,’ she commands and relaxes into the seat.

After a short while...

The cab stops in front of a building bobbling with life and music, with a description “Hot ‘n’ Chillz”. She alights from the cab and gives the driver some tips.

‘See you in a few hours. Later,’ she said, smiling.

‘Ah, thank you o, madam,’ says the cab driver, grinning and revealing his dentition that is coloured in an admixture of brown and yellow and punctured with a missing incisor towards her retracting figure. ‘Kai, this night good.’

In the building…

Cynthia sights her friends as she enters the bar, her two close friends, Stella who is fair-skinned and shares the same size and the almost same height as her and

Moyosore, known as Moyo, who is dark-skinned, plump body size and lips with a beauty spot beside her nose.

'Babe, thank God you're here, I thought you would not be able to come,' Stella says as soon as she and Moyo see Cynthia enter the bar.

'Seriously, you could have just missed the gist as e dey hot,' Moyo adds. She calls the barman, 'Barman, get us all female beer, please.'

Cynthia's gaze gets lost on the barman, she turns to her right to face Stella but her gaze never leaves the barman.

'They have a new bartender? Damn, he's hot,' she says a little too loudly and the barman hears her. He faces her and smiles from where he is, he returns to them with their drinks and serves Cynthia last.

'The name is Josh. The host invited me here, I originally work at "Rhemzy Eat et Bar". You're pretty hot too,' he says as he shifts her portion of the beer to her and flashes her his cute dimple.

Cynthia looks completely mesmerized and charmed. She suddenly jerks and responds, 'arr... Sorry, I am Cynthia. Nice to meet you.'

'Same here,' Josh replies and leaves to attend to other customers.

'Med o, as if we are not existing. What was the meaning of that, Cynthia? Hey, eyes on me, look here girl,' Moyo shakes Cynthia's shoulders. Cynthia finally notices her environment and sees Moyo's questioning eyes.

'What... What are you talking about?' Cynthia asks out of oblivion.

Stella and Moyo crack up, laughing hard.

'Seriously, she doesn't know sha,' Stella says to Moyo then faces Cynthia, 'so Cynthia, you don't even know how weird and off you just acted like no one else here exist but you and your "barman" hmm? Geez, you need to be checked. You don't even acknowledge men sef, so what's with this guy that got you?' she turns in the direction of the barman, 'although honestly, he is cute and hmm... I see why now.'

'Really? Let me see too, what is the "why" you girls are seeing,' Moyo turns in his direction too.

'The eyes,' says Cynthia.

'The arm,' says Stella.

'The lips, oh so...'

'The smile.'

‘The hairy...’

‘Hey ladies! I don’t get what you’re talking about here,’ Moyo flare out.

‘Well, if you don’t get it, then forget about it, girl,’ Stella says and she together with Cynthia burst into laughter, laughing so hard that Stella holds her tummy, ‘my tummy oo,’ she cries out, laughing.

‘Damn y’all, he isn’t that cute sef. I mean he is fine alright but I can’t see any specialty in all those features you girls mentioned. You guys are fucked up, trust me,’ Moyo said.

The duo burst into laughter all over again.

‘How will you see anything about any other man when all you talk about is your “Ben” all the time? Where is he sef? Let’s see what has blinded our friend’s eyes to see other guys,’ Stella says.

‘That’s very true. Where is he? Have you sighted him since?’ Cynthia inquires.

‘No, I haven’t. You know he is the host, he’d have a lot of people to meet, so…’ Moyo trails off looking around.

At a different angle in the building...

A young man, who hosted the party, finally has the time to check out the lady that caught his attention a few moments ago. He calmly assesses the three ladies who seem to be very close.

In the middle is a brown-skinned lady who caught his attention. She is dressed in a simple yet elegant low-neck short gown, firm against her skin. The nude colour of the gown enhances her skin. Her legs are strapped in sandals with heels of the same colour as the gown. The other ladies were pretty cool too as the one on the right has a wine-sparkling short gown on with a big V-neck that shows a pretty good amount of her cleavage, the fair skin made it so bright and eye-catching. Her red painted nails stand out from the open-toes sandals she has on. The lady on the left that he knows very well also dresses beautifully in a pink gown and its length past her knees with a slit that reaches her mid-thigh. She has a pretty ring that sparkles and covers three fingers on her left hand.

'Let's go get introduced,' he says to himself as he rises from the sofa.

As he takes a few steps toward the ladies, a woman stops his track and she smiles brightly. He does not know who she is.

'Hi, Mr Benjamin. I am Mrs Franklin, CEO of Benacruz Luxury Hotels. The party is lit. I would love to have business contract with you, sir. If you don't mind, I believe we can do each other better,' she says.

'Oh right, Mrs Franklin, it is a pleasure to meet you. I would hand you my business card and you can contact my office between Tuesday and Friday then we can talk better. Here, have my card. I have to go,' He steps aside and heads for his destination.

After a few steps...

'You have your eyes elsewhere for the...'

'Hey, ladies,' he cuts in on Cynthia.

The ladies look up and see him. Moyo stands up immediately.

'Oh guys, here is Mr Benjamin. He is the host of the party and my boss. Sir, here are my friends I asked if I can invite, Stella and Cynthia,' Moyo introduces.

'Nice to meet you, Mr Benjamin.'

'Cool to meet you finally.'

Cynthia and Stella say simultaneously.

‘Oh, call me just Ben please and what do you mean by “finally”?’ Mr Ben asks.

‘Oh, Sir, It's nothing serious. Don’t mind my friends, they are pretty naughty,’ Moyo quickly speaks on behalf of her friends.

‘Call me Ben outside the office please. Shall we go have a comfortable seat and start the party?’ He suggests.

The ladies look at each other and nod.

‘Definitely, Ben,’ Cynthia responds with a big smile on her face.

CHAPTER 2: LONG TIME NO SEE

‘Ouch, my head hurts,’ Cynthia whines. She looks around and gets confused.

‘Where the fuck is this place? The curtains… Bedside stool… White lamp… The fuck is going on!’ She shouts then Moyo and Ben rush in.

She looks at them like aliens. Her gaze shifts from Ben to Moyo then she notices her cloth, it is different from last night, she tries to calm down.

‘What the heck is going on? Moyo… Ben… Mind telling me? Please… oh, my head hurts, I can’t reason.’

‘Calm down, you’re fine, nothing happened,’ Moyo says.

Ben just stands, hands in his trouser pockets and watches the scene with amusement, then Stella enters the room with a cup of water and aspirin.

‘Here, it will help reduce the head ache,’ she hands it to Cynthia, ‘you need to go on an alcohol break or something, you recently handle it badly, yesterday’s worse.’

‘You should be grateful to Ben here, he helped us with this exquisite room and assisted us in carrying you here yesterday. We would have all slept together at the bar,’ Moyo says silently to Cynthia.

Cynthia looks up to see Ben boring holes on her skin, ‘thank you Mr... Sorry Ben, sorry for any inconveniences we might have caused,’ Cynthia says shyly, rubbing the back of her neck.

The shy act of Cynthia makes Moyo wonder, *she's never shy before men, hmmm, hope it is not what I am thinking, oh God, let it not be o.*

‘Oh no, you ladies didn't cost me anything, I am glad I could help. Please take your time, Moyo would show you out. Do have a wonderful weekend, ladies.’ Ben replies and leaves the room.

Cynthia and Stella smile and once Ben exits the room they both swiftly face Moyo who seems lost.

‘Oh, can you please shed some light on “Moyo would show you out”, huh?’ Stella inquires.

Moyo frowns her face, giving them a questioning look.

'Nah! No even start your acting sef, tell us the truth, you've been here before? And you never tell us? Shuu! There's God o,' Cynthia says.

'Abi Na, inside life,' Stella adds.

Moyo gasps with her hands on her mouth, 'Ha... I have never been here oo, he just shows me the way out o this very morning before you woke up o. Biko, I no lie o.'

'Hmmm... Or you cornered the poor man confessing your love for him, how you've been daydreaming and having wet dreams, envisioning him on every face, drawing...'

'Ha ah, e don do Cynny. Please, let's get our ass outta here before Moyo decides to report us to her Ben,' Stella whispers the last part and they all burst, laughing.

Sometime, during the week...

Elizabeth catwalks down from the aeroplane at the airport, feeling the cool breeze against her face. She clads in jeans trousers, black camisole with nude overall and black heels, she looks gorgeous with her honey skin completion and she knows it.

Life has treated her badly with her old schoolmates she called friends who had really messed with her emotions and psychology but now she has returned to take revenge which is of great benefit for her. It's going to be so much enjoyment.

She smiles beautifully and adjusts her handbag but she collides with someone and her bags fall. She swiftly looks up, angered.

'You blind or something?' she questions the person she collides.

'Excuse you?' Cynthia says removing her sunglasses and tucking them inside the back pocket of her jeans skirt.

'I know dump people like you would be here trying so hard to get attention. Would you say your sunglasses were so fake that you could not see through them or what? Do you even know who you are speaking with?'

'Wait a minute… Wow!' Cynthia tries to solve the puzzle she's faced with, 'You're Beth? Aina Elizabeth? Med o! Wonder shall never end,' Cynthia tries to remember the last time she saw her, it was certainly that time at her party…

‘Finally, I’d get to sit down,’ Cynthia exhaled as she sat on the cushioned chair with her friends, Moyo and Stella.

They were at an all-white party hosted by Cynthia. The building was blazing with loud music, crowded with people all in different kinds of white.

Moyo passed the cup she had filled with wine to Cynthia, ‘here,’ she said.

‘Thanks, jare,’ Cynthia responded and collected the wine.

They were also in white but only Cynthia’s white combination was epic with her white wig, fingernails, hair rings and eye shadow. If possible, she would had had her eyeballs, lips colour, eyelashes, eyebrows and all that changed to white.

‘But babe, this your party is lit, sincerely. Everything is just sparkling,’ Stella said as she looked around the room the thousand times that evening. The room was just filled with almost all luxuries. Cynthia did spend much on upgrading the room.

‘Am I known for any other thing but “LIT”? Girls, I am Cynthia o, Cynthia Olowoye. If this party is anything but lit, it would not only be a disappointment to my father but to me and even to my generations to come. The reason is this, girls, the money I have right now, even if an earthquake happens and money no longer enters from my dad, it can't get exhausted. This money is too much. Help me spend it. It is burning my hands. Can't my friends feel it? Spend this money for me,' she said, all dramatizing.

'Kpk, omo baba olowo,' Moyo said hailing Cynthia.

Shortly after, *"omo baba olowo"* by Davido was the next song and the room was blazing with song, suiting perfectly into Cynthia and her friend's discussion. Out of excitement, they stood and danced in different styles to the song, singing along as well.

Having a blissful time, they laughed and made a mockery of each other with their dance steps and after what felt like ages of dancing and drinking, Stella noticed a figure in the room.

'Wait, girls. Isn't that Beth? Elizabeth?' Stella said.

'What on earth is she doing here?' Moyo added.

'What audacity!' Stella exclaimed.

'She's even in the dress code. That witch. Backstabber! It is doing me like I should scratch that hair out of her head,' Moyo said through her teeth.

'But really, I thought she is out of Lagos. What then is she doing in here?' Stella asked as she calmed down and tried to reason.

'Girls, just cool down, low lives will always behave like one. Let her just enjoy this party-life whilst she can. That one aside, I can't allow one miserable girl to spoil my mood at my party. Never!'

'Let's party girls,'…

She can also remember they later attacked each other at the party with Beth ready to shove any sharp object down her throat. She shakes her head at the memory and continues what she was saying.

'This is me o, Cynthia, the daughter of… I don't need to do much introduction, you know me better than all this. But wait, you're coming from the airport? And you just spoke to me rashly like that? What the heck are you or what do you trust so much that made you dare talk to me like you just did? I, that can feed you and your generations to come. Are you high?'

Elizabeth laughs at Cynthia's state of confusion, 'your confusion has barely started. I am not back here in Lagos to be a dummy or be played for a fool like you and your shitty ass of friends did but to SHOCK you all,' she smirks, carries her bags and walks out in elegant steps.

Dump folded, Cynthia knows not what to do or the next step to take as her mouth refuses to close or her legs; move.

A middle-aged man stands, holding a placard with the description of "Miss Elizabeth A." on it.

Beth exhales softly, saying to herself, 'I refuse to have a bad day, any day but today. It's a great day, oh yes, it is. Don't wanna be late to meeting my husband-to-be,' she moves closer to the man, introduces herself, enters the car and relaxes on the seat and then smiles.

CHAPTER 3: NOT LOOKING BACK

After a long drive, the cab finally slows down in front of a gigantic gate with the writing of "Chief Olowoye Mansion". Beth smiles brightly, the smile that charms her husband-to-be, she glances around the mansion and takes in its huge form.

The mansion has both big and small buildings in it, a swimming pool by its side and pretty flowers at nice angles. The cab moves and packs rightly in front of the giant door of the big building. The cab man runs to open the door for Beth who never seizes to smile. She carries her bag and presses on the doorbell. She looks back and signals the driver can go.

A man dressed in a white and black shirt and trousers opens the door and ushers her in, she enters the magnificent building and she wows.

'Please wait here, Miss,' he bows slightly and leaves to get Chief Olowoye.

‘No problem, quickly please,’ she responds and finds a seat for herself.

The man returns with an older man in his late 70s, Chief Olowoye, a politician in the ministry of finance. He is tall and dark in completion, very handsome and also rich. He has a smile on his face as he takes gentle steps down the stairs with his arms open wide.

‘Oh, pretty Elisabeth, come, darling, hug me, will you?’ Beth stands and happily moves closer to him and hugs him, ‘I have missed you so much, your smiles, your eyes, your lips and their feel on mine. Oh, I have missed your caresses, and soft morning massages,’ he looks past her and saw her belongings, ‘glad to know you don’t bring much as I have instructed, that's good. I have a wardrobe filled with exotic dresses I know you’d love baby, and the underwear too. I have a lot I'd love to see you try on. But before we go, I would like to introduce you to my family, dear, come,’ he takes her hand and leads her to the sitting room where his sons are waiting.

He has twins, handsome young men who are still in college, second year. The house help has gone to call them as instructed by Chief. They both stand, watching the drama of their father. He has never brought in a woman and displays so much affection for her before, at least none they know of. The woman has the same physical features as their mom, Iyabo Olowoye, plump, tall, honey skin and beautiful. It's quite obvious their dad has a taste.

Mayowa whispers, 'what in the world is the old man doing?'

Muyiwa replies, 'how would I know? He just called us out now obviously,' and pockets into his grey joggers.

'I so wish Cynthia's here. She'd scatter this whole thing for dad, his craziness would clear off.'

'Same here, bro. Oh! Here he comes.'

Meanwhile, outside, Cynthia drives in roughly, she hurries to get inside and pick up what she forgot. She slams the door of her Benz and quickens her steps, she opens the door and freezes. The air in the house feels so terrible, *what on earth is going on?* She thinks to herself.

'Hey, seriously? The fuck are you doing here and holding onto my dad like some parasite? Dad, what's this fake bitch doing here, doing with you?' Cynthia accuses.

'Will you watch your mouth? I was about to introduce her to your brothers before you came in and interrupted us,' Chief replies.

‘Okay,’ she raises her hands and looks in Muyiwa and Mayowa’s direction, ‘alright dad, what’s up? What are you doing with my ex-friend?’

‘Cynthia, Muyiwa and Mayowa, here is Elizabeth, my soon-to-be wife, your ...’

‘What!’ Mayowa exclaims.

‘What the hell dad? What kind of a joke is this?’ Cynthia bursts out.

‘Hey, watch it Wura! Don’t curse in my house. I said she's my soon-to-be wife. You give her as much respect as you regard me.’

‘Ha!’ the boys exclaim.

‘B...but dad, what about mom? Where is her place?’ Muyiwa asks.

‘Imagine, mom is sick in the hospital and here you are taking a new wife,’ says Cynthia.

‘Is mom aware of this decision?’ Mayowa asks also.

‘Look boys, no one is taking your mom’s place, I have only decided to take a second wife and yes, I informed her about this,’ Chief responses.

‘Dad, no. Never. I am not taking this gold digger as a person I would ever respect. You do not know her true identity, dad. She’s a chameleon, I know her better. I am sure she is up to something being here. I met her earlier today, she abused and threatened me, dad, me, your Wura. No way, this can't do. It's either me, Wuraola Cynthia Olowoye or her, you will have to choose,’ she ends breathing heavily.

‘Oh no, Wura. Don’t do this, don’t make me do this. It doesn’t make sense. Elizabeth makes me comfortable and... Just try and accept her.’

Mayowa and Muyiwa look at the scene quietly daring their dad to act wrong.

‘I insist. This is completely insane, I can’t be under the same roof with this thing... Choose now or you lose your daughter forever,’ she breaths.

‘I cannot choose, you guys perform different roles in my life...’

Cynthia, without waiting to hear the rest, picks up her car key which she has dropped when she entered and leaves the living room to her room, storming on the stairs so hard. The twin brothers shake their heads, giving their dad a sad look and leave for their rooms. Cynthia returns to the living room with a suitcase and a handbag and leaves the living room. She heads for the front door sparing no one a look.

Chief never bothers calling anyone back, he's got no time for some spoilt brat.

Later in the evening…

Muyiwa and Mayowa sit at the edge of the hospital bed of their mother then Cynthia enters the hospital room. At the sight of her mother, she breaks, tears drop from her eyes but cleans them immediately. She moves closer to her mother whose usual bright eyes look so lifeless; her long full hair so scanty; her always moistened pink lips so pale and dry.

She moves closer to her mother even more and holds her lukewarm hand, 'mother, are you aware of dad's decision? His decision to take a new wife? Are you in support of it?'

Their mother only stares into the space.

She looks from her mother to her brothers who look so much alike with the twin attire they are in, 'Have you guys asked her?'

The twins look down sad, sorry there has been no response to Cynthia's enquiries. Cynthia notices she might not get any answer, so she gives up. It does not matter after all.

'Come on guys, let's give mama some rest,' she gestures they leave and they voluntarily leave their mother's side and follow Cynthia out. 'what was the doctor's last report on her health? How worse has her cancer gone?' her arms akimbo, she turns to face the boys, her junior brothers.

After that day…

Mrs Olowoye's children throb in and out of the hospital during the next two weeks of their mom's existence. Immediately after the burial, Cynthia detaches from the family completely. Cynthia changes her environment but retains her friends, not like they are going to leave her anyway, it's all for something.

CHAPTER 4: LET'S TALK

Cynthia can be sighted as she catwalks into the reception in her white round-neck long sleeves top and tight trousers covered with Ankara print kimono jacket and the same Ankara print handbag. Her Gucci designer heels of not more than 4 inches click on the tiled floor. She smiles at the receptionist who is already used to her visits and heads straight for her friend's office. She opens the door of the office without knocking and sees Moyo and Chinedu who quickly detaches from each other at the sight of her.

She gaps, 'Oh, I am so sorry, I will just go talk with the receptionist, sorry,' she turns and rushes out closing the door behind her and back to the reception, she slides into the receptionist's counter and smiles at her.

'Hi… how have you been?' Cynthia breaths out.

'Arr... Fine. Did you not see your friend at the office? She hasn't gone out yet, I am sure. Maybe she went to the toilet because I haven't seen her since she resumed this morning. She isn't the type that sneaks around anymore unlike when she first got here. She always finds ways to just hit on guys and go out to eat or go on date or be sick and need to get medicine, flirt...'

'Wait, hum… I saw her at the office actually but she was busy, like really busy, so I just had to excuse her for a while, you know,' Cynthia ends smiling, grateful she could cut in just fine.

'Oh, right, you know I said so, she's been hard-working recently. It's a good thing o but I cannot shake the feeling that it's for the boss she's been working hard for like I said earlier or I was about to say before you cut in. she flirts a lot and I have caught her in different several occasions eyeing our boss but the boss seems to be completely oblivious of the whole situation. I think she wants the boss to notice her; like she's trying hard to get noticed. Besides, who would not want to get noticed by our boss anyway? I mean, he is hot, fair, tall, handsome, rich and cool-headed. It's like he knows the right...'

'Wow… Cynthia, right? Hi,' greets Ben who has entered the reception hall not long ago.

‘Hi,’ she answers right away, anything to get her out of the girl’s grip. How could she forget the girl talks way too much? She moves out of the counter to Ben’s side and faces him.

Having a close look at him, she can see he dresses cool. His white shirt neatly tucked into the ironed black trousers complimented with a sparkling black Italian shoe. He has an expensive wristwatch on his left wrist and a polka-dotted tie fixed on his shirt. Nice. She looks up at him and smiles.

‘Thanks for calling me out here, arr... Can we still call you Ben... here?’ she asks.

‘”We”? Anyway, call me as you wish. Wow, it’s so nice to see you here, I mean, I never knew I would see you so soon after the party, you know. You're here to see your friend, I guess,’ he smiles cutely.

‘Guessed right. I do come here often though to see her, we just don’t meet.’

‘Hmmm, I see. Can I have your contact maybe we can grab lunch sometime?’ he offers.

‘Well, if you’re not in a hurry, we can just grab it now because you're the main person I came to see. If you can please spare a few minutes of your time, I will appreciate that,' Cynthia gives her charming smile hoping it would work, of course, it always does.

'Really? Yes sure, I was originally on my way to have my lunch. So, shall we go now?'

'Definitely.'

'Yeah, this way please.'

After a short drive…

'So, what would you like to have?' Ben asks as he adjusts his seat to be more comfortable.

He has driven to his usual restaurant near his company in his Jeep and has made Cynthia know the bills are on him. A waiter has stood by them ready to take their orders.

'Arr... I will just go for chicken and chips,' Cynthia orders

'Right. Same for me with a bottle of coke, please,' Ben says and dismisses the waiter. He turns to Cynthia and smiles at her.

'So, what would you like to discuss, Cynthia?'

'Okay, I don't have anything to say. I am sorry. I just said that so you can take me away from that girl, I mean your receptionist. She's a hell of a talkative. I am sorry for making you believe I have something important to say.' she says lowly, lowering her head like a child.

This made Ben bursts laughing but he immediately covers his mouth, trying to control it and puts on a serious face.

Cynthia sees this effort; she also bursts out laughing so Ben joins her and they both laugh out loud. They ignore the look of the onlookers.

The waiter returns with their meals, sets them appropriately on the table and leaves.

They both shared a look before they start eating.

'Alright, you have made it clear. Let's just talk about you. Cynthia, I am curious, what do you do?'

She smiles and pushes back her shinning hair, 'well, I am a student, a final year student of accounting,' *Na lie go just kill me,* she says in her thought for she has dropped out the day her mother died. To hell with school.

‘Wow, beautiful! I would not have guessed you’d be in school, you look so much like an independent woman who works hard all by herself. That’s good.’

‘Yeah… I work hard by myself though,’ her mind disturbs her about those lies but she ignores them, willing to impress Ben, ‘I combine school and work together but I mentioned school only the other time because my education comes first for now. I’d graduate soon and I would find a better company to work with.’

‘Impressive. You know, it’s so hard to find a lady that takes her education seriously in this part of the country. You are a wow.’

‘Oh please, stop that. I just love working, can’t help it,’ she gives a sick smile.

She no longer feels comfortable discussing school and work. Two things she’d never do, willing though.

‘This meal is really nice, I never knew a place like this existed. My God! I am almost done sha. It just feels like I should keep eating and it should never end. Thank you so much for this meal, I owe you one.’

‘Yeah, you do. And talking about owing me one,’ he smiles calmly looking into her deep brown pupils, ‘there’s an upcoming dinner I got invited to. It’s a dinner organized for CEOs of numerous companies. We meet, talk business, partner and other things. So, if I am not trespassing, I would so much love to have you go with me… as my plus-one.'

She's dump folded, she drops the fork and then relaxes completely into the seat after cleaning her lips. She doesn't see that coming. Dinner? With those business tycoons? Ben continues to explain the benefits the dinner will be to her if she could attend, plus, it would be a great happiness to him for that will end his search.

'Search? Which search?' Cynthia inquires.

'Oh, I have been meaning to have someone as my plus-one for the party, but now… God has sent an angel my way. I shan't let go.' he ends smiling.

Now I can understand why Moyo is always yelling and singing his name to our ears. Cynthia thinks. A touch on her hand makes her return to reality. She sees Ben giving her an expectant look.

'Oh, I will... I'll think about it. I am not used to these business dinners and all sort of that, so...' she giggles, 'I'd love to think it over. Please give me some time.'

'Oh, that's fine, I will just have your number and we can proceed from there. Here, your pin, please,' he hands her his phone.

Cynthia takes the phone and inputs her phone number. She says she'd love to start going because she has Moyo to return to who has been disturbing her phone with SMS and phone calls. Ben offers to take her because he's also returning to the company. So, they both take their leave.

CHAPTER 5: LOVELY NIGHT

For days, Josh, the bar tender's smiling face, troubles Cynthia. It keeps appearing and reappearing.

'Ha ah, I hope all is well with me o, what's all this na?' she frowns at herself, shakes her head trying all she can to keep the face from returning to her head.

'Grr...' her phone's ringing tone of "Hip Hop Hurray" by Simi interrupts her whining. She first gets carried away by the song, dancing to the tune and singing along then she later rushes to where the phone is and picks it up.

'Hey, hello,' she rushes, breathing hard.

'Hey, Cynthia. This is Ben.'

'Huh…' she looks at her phone, then returns it to her ears and speaks between her teeth, 'oh Ben, good day.'

'Yeah, how are you? Sorry if I have interrupted anything.'

‘Oh, no, it’s fine. You didn’t interrupt that much. I am fine, how are you too? Office work not draining?’

‘Not that much. I would have called you last night but I don’t know your rules and I would not want to be trespassing. Don’t want you to be in some trouble with someone, you know.’

‘I know nothing, Ben. There’s no one you’re trespassing here and I am my boss, nobody’s trouble to be in. You’re free as a bird to call me. But try not to call me during unholy hours, Benjamin,’ she stresses his name.

He laughed out, ‘you had to say it in full. I love how it sounded though, quite peculiar. So, to the point why I called, I just want to have feedback on what we discussed at the restaurant, what do you say?’

And their conversations flow quite well with Cynthia agreeing to meet with him. Ben also suggests to send her a package of what to wear of her favourite colour to the party and Cynthia agrees.

Later that night…

‘Do have a nice night.’ Josh says to the couples that are moving away from his counter, exiting the bar.

Josh resumes his work at "Rhemzy Eat et Bar" a few hours ago. He dresses in black crazy jeans, an Adire shirt that has been ripped at its arm and ties around his neck, a yellow bandana. He looks cute and he knows that, more reason Rhemzy would love to keep him at the night shifts. Cute workers attract customers.

Semilore with the pen name Lorrz is the daughter of Rhemzy's CEO. She's a beauty queen who loves attention. She clads in a white sparkling A-shape skirt that ends at her mid-thigh, a nude transparent shirt tucked neatly into the skirt, held with a tiny black belt. She has her hair down and painted her lips red that stand out against her bleached skin.

She catwalks to Josh's side and smiles, she has always tried her best to look good at the bar ever since Josh resumed in order to seduce him but something always seems to turn him off on her and she knows not.

'Hey, handsome,' Lorrz starts with her usual line.

Josh rolls his eyes at the obvious speaker, he turns to face her and gives her a tight-lipped smile, 'hey, Lorrz, it's you. You look amazing, don't you?' he compliments her effort to show off her boobs through the transparent shirt she has on.

'Oh! You like it? I just got it though together with these earrings and my lingerie I ordered from Jumia last 3weeks and just arrived earlier today. You might want to see it. It looks perfect on me; like it's made for me.'

'Yeah, right,' he ends it already bored. He doesn't like red lips, especially those that look like blood. Arr... It turns him off.

'I should come and show you already, I know you'd love to, let me...' struggling with her shirt.

'Na wetin? Abeg, just hold your peace there. Not interested, thank you. If you don't mind I have important people to attend to.'

He moves to the other side where he has noticed someone standing and on looking at the person it turns out the lady he met at the party he was invited to by the host. Damn, it's Cynthia, how could he forget her name? Her beautiful charming smile has held him captive.

'Hey, Cynthia, right?'

'Hello, good evening. I am Cynthia and I hope you're still Josh.'

'Yeah… I think so,' he giggles, 'what may I get you, Miss?'

'Oh please…' she rolls her eyes, smiling, 'how has the night been for you here? You must be hard working. I love your bandana. Do you have more? Can you spare me one?'

'Hey, calm down, baby, let me respond to everything, okay? My night here has been... well, stressful like every other night. I have a lot of bandanas in different colours,' he losses the bandana he has on him and stretches it towards Cynthia, 'here, you can have this. Where would you want it? Around your hair, wrist, neck like mine, or your bag or you want it has a belt? What do you have on? Oh! It's a gown. I love your dress, by the way'.

Cynthia stretches her wrist forward to indicate she wants it on her wrist. He ties it lightly on her wrist, then holds her hand and kisses the back of her palm as she giggles.

'Wow, your smile is charming, it was what ...' he hears someone calls "barman", so he excuses himself and hurriedly attends to the people who need tending to. After answering the second person, he quickly returns to Cynthia saying she should join him at the counter so that they may have a better discussion.

'What if your boss sees us?' she asks.

'That's if he sees us first, c'mon.'

He returns to attending to people and after it seems there was no more needing his attention, he gives it fully to Cynthia and then realizes her dress is even more beautiful. She has a white armless gown on with fringes at the end of the gown and it all ends above her knees. The neck of her dress shows quite an amount of her cleavage. Seeing this, he licks his lips and knows he will have a lovely night, surely.

They chatted all through the night, laughing and making a mockery of each other till Josh's shift ends. Josh assists slightly-drunk Cynthia to stand and they drag each other out of the bar through the back door. Cynthia decides they crash at Josh's place since he lives alone and it is close. Josh hails a taxi and they highlight at his house. He searches his pockets with one hand, holding Cynthia with the other. He finally finds it after what seems like ages to Cynthia. As soon as she gets inside, she flings off her sandals and swiftly turns to Josh and crashes her lips on his.

The sudden act freezes Josh but then responds to her kisses, smiling that it is a lovely night after all.

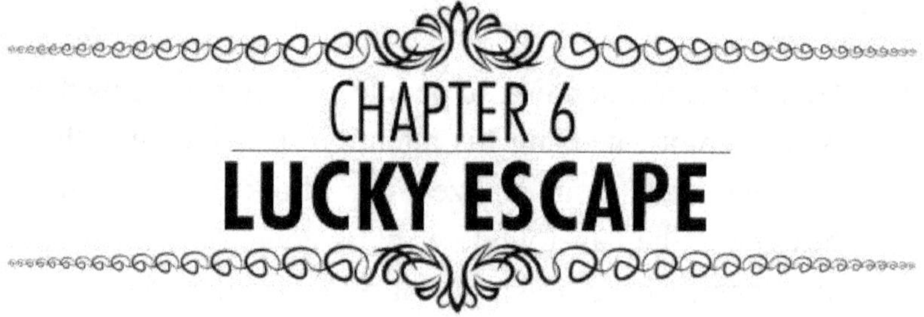

CHAPTER 6: LUCKY ESCAPE

Simi's "Hip Hop Hurray" track, Cynthia's ringtone wakes her from her slumber. She stretches and picks up her call.

'Yeah?' she speaks into the phone.

'Oh, so sorry, didn't know you would be asleep,' Ben apologizes from the other end.

'Really...' she checks the time from her phone, 12:02, 'what!' she sits up, 'Can you please call me back in the next 30 minutes, got to fix something... Yeah, bye,' she hangs up. She looks around, trying to get where she's at.

'Oh,' she smacks her head, 'silly girl. Where's he then?' She looks around, her clothes have been packed beside her bag, she notices he has made her put on his shirt that reaches her mid-thigh. She finally sees the letter Josh has dropped for her on the bedstand stool.

“Hey, princess. Gone to get some things done. You can go to the kitchen and have yourself a coffee or tea. I will be back with our meals shortly,” it reads.

‘Well, cool, isn’t he?’ she moves around the house checking it out, she enters the kitchen and prepares herself a tea. She keeps enjoying the drink and then her phone rings. She checks her caller. Ben.

‘Hi, Benjamin,’ she starts.

‘Hi, Cynthia, I hope you aren’t too busy. You asked I call back in 30 minutes, remember?’

‘I do remember, Ben. How are you today?’

‘Doing great. I want to know if you'd be at home this evening, your package would be delivered this evening, will you be at home?’

‘Yeah, I will. Thank you so much.’

‘Arr...’ Ben hesitates.

‘What do you wanna say? C’mon say it. I give you the courage to speak, Oya, receive courage.’

Ben giggles, ‘Amen, I receive it. I just thought maybe we could have lunch together today. It’s almost lunchtime though and I have been thinking that if where you work is around my company's, maybe we can have lunch together.'

'Wow. So, this is what you're gonna propose and you're breathing so hard. I thought maybe you wanna ask me to cooperate that you'd use me for ritual then we can both share the money,' she jokes and laughs at her silliness.

Ben joins her in laughing.

'Don't mind me though, just being very careful.'

'Okay, I can...yeah, we can have lunch at that restaurant from the other day. Let's make it 2:30. I have some work I want to brush through real quick.'

'Cool by me. Alright, see you later then.' Ben responds and he hangs up.

As Cynthia drops her phone, Josh enters with two plastic bags and has a big smile on his face.

'Princess, you're awake, glory to God. Thought you'd sleep till dusk,' he wraps his arm around her waist her kisses her on her plump lips. 'You look beautiful, even much more in my shirt,' he moves to kiss her on her neck and she tilts her head to give him more access.

She shakes her head and tries to concentrate, 'hey, guy, how far? What do we have in the bags?' she takes the bigger bag and checks what's inside.

Three days after…

Cynthia stands in front of her mirror checking out the dress Ben had sent her. It's a gown that shows a lot of her back. Its length reaches her ankle and the sleeves reach her wrist. It's a velvety-grey colour. The package has a very beautiful diamond necklace and matching earrings. The shoes have silver stones all around them, making them glitter. She wonders if she will be able to give Ben what he wants. He's spending too much on her.

The dinner goes well with Ben all over her. His right hand is on her low back which is completely exposed due to the type of dress it is. She has arrived at the party in her Benz and Ben was shocked to realize she owns something of such. Ben introduces her to lots of businessmen and women as he had promised. They return to Ben's place in his car, promising Cynthia he'd send his staff to get hers.

Cynthia looks at herself in the mirror the second time that evening but in Ben's bathroom this time as she removes the hair clips and pins from her hair, then splashes water on her face. She checks the mirror again and touches her lips where Ben has kissed her earlier. His face in her memory is messing with Josh's face. It bothers her.

Ben walks into the bathroom to check on her, she's spending more time in the bathroom than he expects. Seeing her looking gloomy in the mirror makes him bother too.

'You okay, baby?' he stands behind her, holding her waist and massaging it a little.

She stares at Ben through the mirror, 'I... I am fine, just that... I need clarifications, Ben. What...why are you doing this? The free lunches, super affection, this dinner, the motherfucking expensive apparel and accessories, I don't get it. Come clean with your intentions, please,' she has turned and has held him by his shoulders.

Ben still holds her by her waist but more lightly now. 'Okay. I like you, Cynthia, a lot. So far, every moment we've spent together has been awesome. If only you knew how much those little lunches we had together and phone calls meant to me, they are the peak of my days. You make me happy, Cynthia. I would love to make you mine,' he says softly and leans down to kiss her but she moves back, pushing him slightly by his shoulders.

Cynthia tries to reason with Ben but he is bent on having his way with her that night. Ben tries all he could on her, she too fights with her might, not willing her soul to sleep with him or in the house. She struggles so hard and once Ben's hands are off her mistakenly, she escapes his grip. She runs down the stairs, straight out of the house. She glances around the compound and rushes toward her car. Fear grips her when she hears footsteps coming from the house but luckily, the car key is left in the car. She gets herself out of the compound like the ground of the compound is burning her feet.

She hears Ben calling her name, saying he's sorry and all but she doesn't pause, slow down or look back. She is grateful she could escape the lion's den.

CHAPTER 7: THE BARGAIN

Moyo's desk phone rings and she picks it up.

'Can you please come to my office when you're free? I want to see you for a bit.' The voice booms.

'Oh, s... sure, sir.' she stutters.

'Thank you,' says the voice.

Ben just called; her boss, her crush. She's happy he has called. Who knows what he called for? Maybe he has finally gotten her signals and maybe has fallen for her. Seems her prayers are getting noticed and are gradually being moved to the answer box.

'Yes!' she squeaks.

She dances joyfully from left to right in her office corners. After a short while, she adjusts her dress, stands straight, and moves to the door. She tries to tame her smile but it keeps getting wide.

As she's about to open her door, she bursts out laughing again. She then turns, leaves the door side, and holds the table for support.

‘Geez, I can’t help it.’ she fans herself with her palm, smiling.

‘Damn girl. Come on, sit first.’ she finds her way to her seat and sits, ‘now breathe and think.’ She says to herself, as instructed by herself takes in a huge amount of breath and slowly releases it. She knows just how to calm herself.

‘He would know you’re desperate if you show up right away or don’t you think? That’s true, he might also see me as a jobless girl. Very true… let me just calm down first she soliloquies.

As she takes face wipes from her bag, someone enters her office.

‘Hey, baby…’ her colleague says.

Chinedu, Moyo’s colleague with whom she sins and keeps it secret. They have been having an affair for a while now.

‘Ha, Chinedu. I have told you times without a number to always call me before coming over. How is that so hard to do, huh?’ Moyo laments.

‘Calm down, honey. I have tried your number now but you didn’t pick up. I have been craving your touch so much all day that it’s driving me crazy. That is the harmless reason I have decided to come and… thank God that the coast is clear. Come here.’ he says and tries to pull Moyo closer to him; Moyo yanks her wrist off his.

‘I didn’t know you’ve been calling me, but right now, our boss just called and he asked to see me, so I am preparing to see him. Maybe that’s why I did not know you’ve been calling. So...if you will excuse me, I have a call to respond to,’ Moyo says with haste.

Chinedu refuses to move, giving her a knowing look. He keeps quiet and smiles charmingly at her, passing a message Moyo understands so well.

‘Oh, let’s make it quick then,’ she turns to hold the table, shooting her legs backward.

‘Not so fast, babe, come here,’ he pulls her hands and gives her kisses, massaging her waist. She breaks the kiss and speaks.

'We have to be fast o, Chinedu. Honestly, I don't want the boss to start saying anything that's not good about me being ...'

Chinedu keeps giving her kisses around her face and neck which makes her muffle her words and tilt her head backward.

Shortly after…

'Come in,' Ben says with his head facing the laptop before him, checking out some goods.

'Good afternoon, sir. Sorry, I am just coming, I had a lot to quickly take care of.'

On hearing her voice, he looks up and smiles.

'Oh, that's not a problem though. Let's seat on the couch, shall we?' he gestures and moves to the couch.

Ben, as they sit, takes a while to just smile and look at Moyo in the eyes. This act gives Moyo crazy ideas. *This must be it, he has finally fallen,* she thinks, also smiling back.

‘So, I would like to say thank you for honouring my invitation to the party I hosted a few months back and for also bringing your friends to grace the occasion. Sorry, I am just showing my appreciation,’ he says calmly.

‘Oh, not at all sir, it’s all fine,’ she waves it, eager to hear what he has to say, what her ears have been hitching to hear since she started praying about Ben loving her.

‘Thanks, so... I met one of your friends, Cynthia, not long after the party, and... we clicked. We started chatting and going out together, having fun and all that but something happened, I fucked up, I acted immaturely and out of impulse which is so wrong and offensive. It angered her and she cuts me off. I don’t know how to apologize to her, I haven’t known her to that aspect but, honestly, I would love to keep her company with me, you know, as a businessman, I have to live in peace with all men, even the Bible says so. So, Moyo...’ he calls, taking Moyo's hand.

The touch makes her shake and jerk back to reality. She stopped listening after the mention of the name Cynthia. She is not feeling so well, and the feeling isn’t a good one, it's bitter and deadly. She has suddenly developed an illness and her breathing pattern has changed slightly.

She tilts her head and smiles sheepishly at the contact, trying to cover her ranging mind.

'Y-Yes Ben.' her voice shakes.

'Please, can you assist me and apologize to Cynthia for my behavior? It was just a childish act from me, do tell her I would not try it anymore, I promise,' Ben says slightly sounding desperate.

Moyo shifts back a bit, getting irritated. 'So, you want me to apologize to her on your behalf, right?' Ben nods, 'But, what's your offense, I'd love to know.'

'Hmm... I don't want to share it, sorry, Moyo. It is a stupid move on my part; just help me out here. I am getting miserable. I'd so love it if you can help.'

'Okay, sir, no problem.'

'Really!' he exclaims joyfully and hugs her 'oh, thank you so much, Moyo, I will forever be grateful, I owe you one if you do this for me.'

CHAPTER 8: WHO KNOWS WHO

'Sir, I'd like to see you,' Moyo requests.

'Oh yeah, do come in,' Ben says and as Moyo enters, he checks her out for a few seconds. She clads in an armless white shirt with a very low neck, tucked in a high-waist black skirt.

'Sir, I have apologized to her, pleaded with her and other things but she said you didn't offend her at all. So...' she shrugs.

'That's not so. I am sure she just doesn't want you to bother. I must have angered her deeply then. I must...'

'Calm down Ben.'

It shocks Ben that Moyo is already by his side, addressing him with his name in the office, also with her palm on his chest in her own attempt to calm him. He looks at her and tries to understand what she's saying.

'Cynthia can be like that sometimes but I know just how to make her forgive you completely, holding nothing back. You have to trust me, huh?'

'Okay, help me out here.'

'But on a condition.'

'Yes? Which is?'

She slowly undoes his shirt buttons which shocks Ben.

'Ha ah, sorry? What's this?'

'I have always wanted you, Ben, but if I can't, I would love to have just a night with you and that would be it. It's going to be a win-win after all, you want Cynthia and I want you. You're even of a higher percentage here. Think of it Ben, it's not like I am that bad.' she says softly, her voice caressing his skin like velvet.

Ben, getting drowsy, says nothing but looks into Moyo's eyes, lost in the pool of her brown pupil. Moyo takes the advantage of Ben's incapability to resist her and undoes the rest of the buttons of his shirt, slowly touching his lips with hers.

Gradually, she pushes Ben backward, aiming at the cushioned chair in his office as they kiss and as it seems his feet have hit the chair, Ben's desk phone rings, jacking him to reality. He moves out of Moyo's hold and walks to his desk to pick up the call.

‘Speak’, he says as he struggles to button up his shirt.

‘Ask the woman to come in the next 7 minutes,’ he commands and drops the call.

He remains quiet for a few minutes, trying to take in what almost just happened. He takes a deep breath and exhales, ‘Moyo, we can’t do this, it is not appropriate.

On hearing this, Moyo gets bothered, she was happy she was getting what she wants after all for a little or zero favour. She has always admired him, almost everything about him and it's such a pain she's losing him to Cynthia; that spoilt arrogant child. Moyo pulls a sad face on and pouts.

‘At least not here, or now for that matter. Here is an office, let’s keep it professional, okay?’ Ben ends holding Moyos face which is already brightened up with a smile.

‘Oh, of course, sir. “Professional” is my middle name. So where would you want we...’ her voice fades off suggesting Ben should talk.

‘Yeah, the hotel down the road here would do, Skyroof Hotel and Suits or whatever it’s called by 7 tonight, how about that?’ He suggests.

‘Any of your options is cool by me sir.’ she smiles and straightens her skirt. ‘I’d take my leave now sir. See you soon,’ she winks.

‘Bye. And you can hint the secretary to allow the woman in on your way out.’

‘Yes, boss,’ she nods and closes the door, smiling.

A week after…

Moyo highlights from a cab with her emerald green handbag and matching shoes and belt, she has a white gown on with her hair packed up in a messy bond. She enters a mall needing to fill up her fridge, it's getting empty and since Cynthia has sent her some money to fill it up, why won't she? She picked both necessary and unnecessary things like she usually does, even those things she ends up throwing away, she still gets them, it's not her money after all.

On entering the mall, she turns right to the beverage section. After a while of picking up almost everything on the shelves, she starts to head to the cashier but unluckily, she jams an angry woman.

'Ha ah, madam, you no see?' Moyo asks irritated.

'It's you and offspring no see. Na me you dey follow talk like that? Or you want me to... Wait a minute. Isn't this the bastard we are looking for here?' the angry woman said and one of her bodyguards confirms Moyo's picture on his tab.

'Oh, it's the idiot my husband cheats on me with? You this dirty girl from the slum. Do you think you can come here to the city and mess up as you do at that dirty village of yours? Oh, you think my husband has a cool-headed woman? I don't know what you think that makes you feel free and okay to do shit and still have the guts to walk out of your house but you must be completely dumb. You dirty piece of shit!' the woman says with so much anger.

It amazes Moyo how her simple question could get such an angry answer. She looks at the woman who has just abused her like she is a nobody. The woman puts on a bubu gown made with Kampala, her sandals have little heels behind them, which gives her a little more height making her tower over Moyo.

‘Ha ah, madam calm down. See me well, I look dirty to you? Or what’s with all these accusations ...’ she could not finish before the angry woman runs out of patience and instructs the bodyguards to drag her out of the mall.

‘Alaye... How far na? Leave me jare... Na which kind thing be this Na? Leave me joor... Ha ah... You people dey craze ni...’ Moyo keeps shouting non-stop at the top of her voice not grasping what is going on.

‘Turn her to face me,’ the angry madam instructs the bodyguards holding Moyo. ‘Listen, slut.’ she says with so much venom, ‘Let me clear this puzzle for you because I know you're too dumb to do that yourself. Look at me very well, I am Efe, Chinedu’s wife. Does that ring a bell?’

And that short introduction rings severally in Moyo’s head, and that sorts the puzzle. Her eyes widen and she wishes she can just get swallowed by the ground at that moment.

‘Answer me, bitch!’ Efe yells.

Moyo gets frightened and her legs lose their grip on her causing her knees to collide with the ground.

‘Ah... Yes, ma, it does o...’ Moyo shakes vigorously, answering Efe.

‘Good, so you can respect, too late darling. Boys! Beat this shit up. Let’s give her a memory she shall live to tell its tale,’ Efe says and smirks.

The bodyguards beside her beat the hell out of her. There are onlookers; people that know her, her neighbors, co-workers, club mates, and all saw her. Some just point fingers while most take videos of the scenario as whispers and laughter fly.

Efe instructs the boys to stop when she seems satisfied.

‘This, Moyin or whatever the hell your name is, is just a friendly visit. I don’t want to ever smell you near him again, I hope you understand. See you in hell,’ she turns to her right and heads to her car parked outside the street.

CHAPTER 9: YOU'RE EXHAUSTED!

'Geez... what the fuck happened to you?' Stella asked checking out Moyo's wounded face.

Moyo has been hiding her face for days from her friends. She has taken a sick leave from the office till a makeover can cover her bruises left. She doesn't want her friends questioning either.

'Eh, so it is true. It's you after all. I have been defending you, fighting my online friends that it can't be you. Who is the woman sef?' Cynthia said surprised.

'What are you talking about?' Stella asked curiously.

'Oh, you don't know? She's everywhere on social media. The video shows that our darling friend here was beaten by a woman's thug. The woman's physic is so intimidating and her bodyguards too. No be small thing. Moyo, talk to us, what happened? How would you allow that woman to mess with you, a fine Lagos babe? She really did mess up your fresh skin that I am always jealous of. Chai! Na how you take do am sef?' Cynthia ends facing Moyo.

How manage! She used to be jealous of my skin? With that beautiful skin of hers? What a new way to mock me... Moyo thinks.

Moyo exhales deeply, 'it's actually not true, it... it's a false accusation, yes. She misunderstood something but she has apologized and we have settled things and...'

'Taa, Na who you dey sell that for? Gbe joor,' Cynthia interjects, 'You would have made her make a public declaration that the issue was a mistake and you would have been rich because I know you would have made her pay you lots of money for the physical damages she caused on your face. So don't even go there at all...'

'Eh, wait sef, is me you? Is you me? Or what's…' Moyo cuts already standing against Cynthia.

'Hey, hey, don't even start any fight o. Please stop. I no get energy jare,' Stella interrupts tiredly not ready to see her friends in each other throats. 'Moyo, I hope you visited the hospital or at least the clinic. This wound must have been a serious one that it's still this scary after how many days?' She checks Moyo's wound.

'You know she doesn't like going to the hospital or taking drugs at all,' Cynthia says already out of her fight mood. 'Besides, these wounds are already healing up na. We all know any wound scares you, ordinary mosquito bites sef makes you nauseous. Abeg, exaggeration,' Cynthia dismisses Stella.

'Anyway, have you eaten anything today? Let me prepare you spag-jollof, the way you love it. I know you will have the ingredients, you always do,' Stella throws to Moyo who nods like a puppy at the sight of bone.

A few days later…

'Sorry, not enough fund,' the cashier of "TWO-4-SEVEN Mall" returns Cynthia's master card for the third time.
Cynthia swallows her saliva and quickly changes the card to the last one she owns and gives the cashier.

'That's Diamond, it definitely gonna be that,' she takes a deep breath, saying silent prayers with her fingers crossed.

And when the cashier finally withdraws her card and smiles, she smiles back too but it's only for the moment. She carries her shopping bags in both hands and walks to her car. She drops the shopping bags in the back seat and sits at the driver's side. She exhales deeply.

After a short drive…

For more than 15 minutes, she rests her head against her hands on the stirring wheel after she has driven herself to her apartment. She is deep in thought, completely lost. She finds it so hard to believe it, she can argue it, or has she been robbed? Just like a prodigal son, she felt so convenient about living alone and spending as much as she can without working or doing anything to gain at all. The thought of the money she spends getting exhausted has never for half a second crossed her mind. Damn, she feels so loveless, without breath, so dead.

'How Cynthia, how? Damn girl, you're so dumb, you're quite pretty but so dumb. Your dumbness is so much more than your beauty. No wonder dad didn't bother looking for you, you're of no use to him or his business and he couldn't even use you in a marriage contract for his business for he knows his going to lose instead. Haaa...'

'Hey Princess.'

She's cut by someone saying and on looking at the person, the person turns to be Josh.

Seeing Josh made her eyes water even more.

'Wow girl, come on. Did anyone hurt you?' Josh asks with all tenderness.

'I wish, I so wish Josh.'

'Okay, what's up then? Wait sef, come here, let us go inside. I have been calling your line that I may inform you that I am coming with lunch,' he helps her out of her car and also with her shopping bags.

He drops all he has on his hands to find Cynthia's house keys from her purse that she has said and when he founds it, he opens the door. Cynthia enters, gripping the bags he has dropped, he moves into the dining to drop the lunch he brought.

Cynthia looks completely melancholy, too moody for Josh to take. He moves to the seat she sits and holds her face up.

'Princess, tell me, what's going on? You're not making me feel good. Is what happened that bad?' he enquires.

Cynthia shakes her head side by side, she uses the back of her palm to dry her tears. She tries to speak but fresh tears roll down again. Josh sees this and hugs her, wrapping his hands around her head against his chest.

'It's going to be okay, Princess,' he whispers.

But Cynthia knows it never going to be. Not anytime soon.

The next day…

Moyo and Stella enter Cynthia's apartment after so much bothering from Josh to check up on Cynthia, whose words refuse to come out of her mouth. Moyo dresses in a chiffon short gown and Stella in palazzo trousers with a crop top. They are dresses Cynthia got for them.

Moyo doesn't look happy to see Cynthia at all but Josh's bother would not let her be. *She always has men wrapped around her fingers. They all bow at her feet.* This is a thought she has entertained severally. She has been furious that Ben who she's also trying so hard to get, has easily been caught by Cynthia's charm. It pains her so much.

Josh has excluded himself so that the girls can talk. He doesn't go to the bar anymore; he has been sacked. Lorzz, just like Potiphar's wife, framed Josh for sexual harassment, and as the daddy's favourite, she was able to get Josh to lose his job. He's not really on a hunt for a job though, he has fallen in love with a money bag.

'Girl, what's up with this mood of yours, Cynny? Do you have any idea how draining this is? Look at Josh, it's exhausting. Just talk already,' Stella starts as she sits by Cynthia's side.

'I... I am…' Cynthia finds it so heavy to say.

Moyo looks at Cynthia from afar, resenting her, 'come on, we have been here for almost 30 minutes. Say something na,' she forcefully said, biting her tongue.

'I am broke,' Cynthia rushes and covers her face with the scatter cushion she has with her.

Stella and Moyo exchange glances and look back at Cynthia. Moyo's interest skyrockets and she moves closer to the nearest empty seat to her.

'What did you just say? Calm down, Cynthia and explain, please,' asks Moyo.

CHAPTER 10: PARTY AT THE POOL

'We need to be very, I mean extremely strategic about this one o. If we fail lasan, any mistake like this, na kiri kiri be that o. No break no jam,' Raphael warns.

Raphael is a friend to Josh who has more experience in robbing. It has been months that Cynthia and her friends together with her boyfriend had resolved to steal than go back to the street or return to her dad like the prodigal son but as wise as she is, she'd rather die.

Never will I do something like that, a house where that thing of a human called Elizabeth is the head. Over my dead body. She had said.

Moyo has assisted the group in robbing Ben's company twice now and Stella has done well too to pave way for their gang to rob big stores in the market. Cynthia herself uses the influence of her father to rob numerous rich folks.

Their gang is made up of 6 members. Raphael, a black tall, and muscular guy, also known as Ralph, is their director. Dunsin, a lanky guy with big eyeballs is their computer guru, he can hack the hacker itself, he knows well about internet fraud. Stella is their seductress. Josh is the master planner. Moyo and Cynthia are more of informants and human relations.

Two weeks ago, they have been planning to rob the house of a politician they heard has a safe in his mansion. So, they are at Cynthia's apartment, where they do meet for their meetings mostly.

'Well, we just have to come up with a solid plan, maybe we can create an ambush on his way home, burst his car tyres, break his side glasses, mess up with his ribs and make him confess how to go about the alternative for his lock or he *kukuma* follow us to his house, use his palm itself to unlock it himself and there, the glory becomes ours, see?' Dunsin says with a huge grin on his face.

Every other person in the room looks at him with an obvious "not interested" look directed at him.

'We clearly aren't as stupid as you are, Dunsin darling,' Stella says to Dunsin with a fake smile and faces others, a plan please.'

‘As in a realistic plan,’ Ralph says emphasizing the word “plan”.

‘The safe’s lock is handprint, Abi?’ Josh asks no one in particular.

‘Yes, Josh,’ Moyo answers.

Cynthia eyes Moyo immediately after her response. Moyo has attempted shamelessly to seduce Josh which irritates him, even every other member of the gang knows about it.

‘If that’s the case, we have to look for a way to get his palm prints...’

‘Yeah, maybe through a handshake or we serve him food or he slaps one of us so we can then scan anything we see him touch or something,’ Ralph cuts in.

‘Hmmm, I like that slapping part, let’s get Dunsin to irritate him, maybe the slap would reset his head,’ Stella jokes and they laugh except Josh who has his hands on his jaw, thinking away.

‘Wait, what if we get a slap on our cloth, or a pet or a...wait sef, Sebi you said he likes ladies,’ he directs to Cynthia who is sited beside him in a transparent shirt and bum short. He has one of his palms on her lap.

‘That’s accurate,’ Cynthia responds.

‘So, I think it would be completely easy to get his print if we use a female figure to make him touch something they have on which can be anything, do we know anything that turns him on?’ Dunsin asks.

Ralph, answers, ‘a naked sexy body like that of our ladies here, especially, our mummy Cynthia would turn anyone on.’

‘No no, don’t even mention her name. She can’t be our sexy goddess. Your eyes off, Ralph. I dey warn you o, control that your yeye eyes o,’ Josh points a finger at Ralph.

‘Why is Stella traveling for a whole week sef? Can’t you come and help us then return or we kukuma shift the operation time,’ Josh suggests.

‘No, oga. No shifting. I can't wait to spend on this babe here, Stella, so she can stop washing me. I need to show her I can get any girl I want,’ Ralph says licking his lips as he says so, his eyes on Stella who mocks him instead.

Cynthia giggles, ‘but darling, it's not like I would have sex with him o, chill na.’

‘Nah, you're for me to touch and feel alone, no one else, understood?’ he says lowly to Cynthia, rubbing her thighs and kissing her nose as she laughs even more.

‘But, I am available now, or aren't I sexy enough?’ Moyo suggests.

‘Not that you are not sexy… you are fine o, in fact very beautiful more than this coconut face called Stella,’ Ralph says and pokes Stella’s head then Stella makes a sound with her hand colliding with Raphael's back.

‘Ouch, but, Moyo, your sexiness no plenty like that. Your figure isn't that provocative, unlike Cynthia's wide hips do make one go crazy, even Dunsin with his dead brain no go wan tell me he never had a wet dream about her,’ Ralph ends and immediately has a shoe hits his shoulders.

‘Okay, something drop for my mind now, the next party the man will surely attend will determine her dressing, if it’s dinner, she wears a dinner gown, if it’s a business meeting then she gets to dress casually, if it’s ... Shey you get like that Josh,’ Josh nods, ‘oya, Dunsin check am,’ Stella prompts.

Dunsin turns to his laptop and gets busy trying to know the next party scheduled for the unfortunate politician.

A few days after…

Cynthia catwalks out of the pool, dripping wet, and the light from the buildings surrounding the pool in contact with the water on her skin, made her skin glow.

Yeah, it's a pool party. After a lot of debates and fights and reasoning, Josh has agreed Cynthia can go.

I cannot have Cynthia been touched by that dirty man's hand, who knows where those hands have been? He had said to make them have a change of mind and obviously, he failed.

Cynthia, make a promise, pinky swear that you would not betray our love for that man, huh? Promise? He had made Cynthia promise him to not overdo with the whole tactic. He had pleaded that Cynthia should not do anything with that man to get back at him if he might have offended her that he might not be able to get over it.

Ralph, Josh, and Dunsin sit in front of the laptop placed on the table and they watch Cynthia's movements. Josh has had Dunsin attach a video device to the necklace she has on so that they may know what's going on and if they might need help.

Moyo has offered to drive Cynthia to the arena the party holds. She remains in the car, waiting for her to return so that she may drive her back home.

Cynthia grabs a drink from one of the servers and catwalks to her target. When she realizes she has caught his attention, she smiles and slows down with her steps, making seductive moves. When she finally reaches where he's at, the man has already sent away the girls he holds before and opens his arms wide for Cynthia. Cynthia sits on his lap and leans into him, giving him the drink she has with her.

‘Hey, popsy. You look finer than you seem in the pictures we see,’ Cynthia starts, smile never leaves her lips which she has painted nude. The colour is a similar colour to her bikini.

The chief grins so widely and spanks Cynthia’s butt which is covered in bikini pants and squeezes it hard. Cynthia notes she has what she wants, it's time for her to start calculations on how to her ass out of there.

He leans in to kiss her but she turns her face and he ends up kissing her cheeks.

'Hey, don't tell me you're shy, you've fucking turned me on baby, let me, allow me to spoil you with anything you will need, no, want. With everything that can ever cross your mind e, just allow me eh...' as he says this, he wraps his arms around Cynthia's waist and pulls her closer wanting to feel her lips, they call onto him.

Cynthia panics for that scene reminds her of the incident at Ben's place. Quickly, she stands automatically making the chief wonder what he might have done.

'Oh no chief, you have done nothing wrong. I think I have taken the wrong drink whilst at the pool, I quickly need to use the restroom, please. I will be back before you know. Excuse me.'

The Chief nods smiling, not bothering to cover the tent his trousers have made, takes another drink and sips from it, waiting. Only God knows when he's going to wait.

CHAPTER 11: TWINS' BANTER

Evang. Mrs. Folayan grips the stirring-stick hard as she stirs the jollof rice in the pot on the gas cooker. She has a light round neck top on a white Ankara wrapper hanging low on her waist. After a while, she covers the pot then she starts to sing as she gets the other ingredients for the Jollof from the cabinets.
Her husband, Rev. Folayan enters the kitchen and sights his wife singing, something she loves to do, moving side to side to her song. He smiles, moves forward, and places one of his hands behind her.

'Iya Ibeji, you so much love singing, you'd get a chance to sing anywhere,' he says.

'Ah, Oko mi. Good morning, olowori mi,' she kneels in greetings.

'Nde nile. You shall be prosperous. More wisdom, more understanding for you in Jesus's name. More respect for you as you give me. How was your night?' He helps her to stand up.

'It was good, you know very well that I love to sing now, you know,' she responds as she attends to the meal she is preparing.

'Yes, I know very well. You know I do tell you that it is your voice that first attracted me o, I was just going my way o and your sonorous voice refused to let me have peace, it sounded in my head for days...'

'That you had to come looking for the voice owner, and that's me, arewa, Abake Feyikemi, Aya Folayan,' she cuts in ending the story with action, moving up and down the kitchen aisle, as she holds the tip of her top so high that gives her a proud stance.

'Wow, my queen, come here, your pride is too much, kilode? Na only you Waka come?' he jokes and they both laugh.

As she turns to check out what she's cooking, John walks inside the kitchen with a hard face and Jude, hot on his heels.

John moves close to their dad, 'Dad, warn Jude o, he has been disturbing me,' he reports.

‘Ha, me, disturb you? Fear God o. Wasn’t I just asking for your phone? Abi I cannot ask for your phone again? You are just selfish,’ Jude returns.

‘Is it your phone ni? Is it not my phone? Or am I the one that ask you to spoil your phone? And you will not let me use my phone peacefully because I ...’

‘E don do, o ti to. Stop all this your cat and rat fight jare, it is annoying,’ their mom cuts on John.

‘It’s Jude,’ John cries

‘It’s John,’ Jude tackles

‘It’s Jude.’

‘It’s John.’

‘Will you boys stop all already? Why would you be yelling with your mother and me amongst you? Nonsense,’ their dad scolds the young lads.

‘That reminds me, Jude,’ their dad calls, ‘go to my bedroom, you will see ₦500 on the bed stool, take it and get me a recharge card, MTN 200,’ he instructs.

Jude rushes off and then Rev’s phone rings, he leaves the kitchen to pick up the call.

'Why do you and your twin brother always find things to fight about, huh? Why can't you lend him your phone anyway?' Mrs. Folayan asks John.

'Mom, you don't know that stubborn boy at all. Once he gets the phone, hell may break loose before he returns it. No o,' he pauses. 'there was a particular day last week, not long after his phone broke down, he took my phone without my consent and held it for the whole day. A lot of appointments I had planned were aborted. I had to start apologizing to the people I disappointed the next day. I was pained that day eh.' he ends.

'Sorry, my boy. He is so stubborn, sorry, Oko mi Kehinde. Ẹ̀jìrẹ́ ará ìṣokún.

Ẹdúnjobí

Ọmọ ẹdun tíí ṣeré orí igi

Ọ́-bẹ́-kẹ́ṣẹ́-bẹ́-kàṣà,

Ó fẹsẹ̀ méjèèjì bẹ sílé alákìísa;

Ó salákìísà donígba aṣọ.

Gbajúmọ̀ ọmọ tíí gbàkúnlẹ̀ ìyá,

Tíí gbàdọ̀bálẹ̀ lọ́wọ́ baba tó bí i lọ́mọ.

Wínrinwínrin lójú orogún

Ejìwọ̀rọ̀ lojú èmi...' she's reciting twins' eulogy for her son when she saints a burning meal. 'Ha! My food o...' she turns swiftly and attends to the meal.

John giggles and his mom smacks his head lightly making him laugh out.

'Oni yeye. Go get the plates to the dining room and set the table. Let's have breakfast.'

Later that day…

The Folayan's family is the family that pastors a very big church in Lagos. Rev. Dr. Folayan and Evang. Mrs. Folayan has a girl of 20 years, Miracle, who is currently at the University of Ibadan, and twins boys of 16years, Jude and John.

The church they head, has planned to have a crusade on that day in the evening. There would be a rally before everyone converges at the crusade point. Rev. Folayan has been making a series of phone calls, making sure things are in place.

He dresses quickly and while trying to fix his cufflinks, his wife enters and she helps him with it.

‘So, where would you be going first?’ his wife asks while fixing the cufflinks.

‘I have called the committees that we are to meet at the church auditorium this morning for any last-minute changes, from there I will...’ he remembers something, ‘I will have to send some messages to the evangelists and prophets we have invited, just a good morning and safe trip message, or what do you feel?’ he asks for his wife’s suggestion.

‘I think that’s cool, it will be appreciated.’

‘Thanks, love. The meal was wonderful too, we should eat that again soon or don’t you think?’ he raises his eyebrow. He holds his wife's waist and kisses her on both cheeks and bides her farewell before leaving the room to the sitting room.

He saw his sons in the sitting room fighting over the channel they’d play.

‘Boys.’ he calls out, 'Make sure you get to church early for the rally, don’t be late, don’t disappoint God and man, okay?’

‘Okay, sir.’

‘Yes, papa,’ John and Jude say simultaneously.

'Good, I am off boys, be good.'

As soon as the sound from their dad's car fades away, they return to fight over the channel to play till John gives up. He takes his phone and leaves the sitting room where his twin brother may eat the whole TV as he has said.

Their mom dresses in blue attire with black flat shoes and a black handbag to match. As she fixes her glasses in their case, she instructs John to make sure all the home appliances are switched off before leaving the house with his brother.

CHAPTER 12: EXECUTION

'Alright, my gentle folks, let's get this thing started, shall we?' Josh says.

'Aye, aye, captain,' responds Ralph alone.

They are in the operation room as they had named it in Cynthia's apartment. The room is just with just a headlight that faces down in the middle of the room. The room has different kinds of gadgets and weapons set on a very large table. Moyo stands between Ralph and Stella on one side of the table and Cynthia stands beside Josh with Dunsin on the other side.

They all dress in complete black attire with hand gloves and face masks which are yet to be worn, hanging around the belt hole of their trousers.

'Stick strictly to the plan and all will be well with you,' Josh encourages.

'And if not, na Sango go kill you o,' Ralph adds.

'Let's wear our gadgets, please and pick the appropriate weapon, no go do pass yourself o. Moyo, I dey warn you now o, no carry the one wey no go allow you move o. I talk my own,' Dunsin warns.

They start putting on their appropriate and necessary gadgets and weapons as they have planned.

Meanwhile…

'Start dressing now, I won't tell you again o. I am locking the door and turning off every appliance in this house once I step out. Maybe I would have to lock you in,' Jude warns.

'What is it sef? I can lock the door myself Na. What's there you're shouting all about gan?' John responds, annoyed.

'Oh, you don't know? The key was given to me, I have to be the one to return it. So, get that flat smelly ass of yours out of your bugs-filled bed and get ready. No say I no tell you o,' Jude warns again.

'If you're not careful yourself, I will take the key and lock you inside the house and go church. No push me o.'

'Ha ah, enipe? Sir? You don't even know what youre saying. How on earth would you lock me in when it's you that hasn't shifted a bit since mom and dad left? You stuck to your phone throughout, smiling like a jellyfish over the phone,' he takes few steps closer to John, 'Na who you dey chat sef? Abi Na yahoo yahoo you dey do?' he peaks into John's phone.

John swiftly turn his phone away fearing Jude would snatch it and says, 'hey dude, you wan enter my phone?'

'Wait, first, it's not dude, it's Jude, and… Na who be Rose? Wait o, is it Rose, ọmọ Adejare from our church? Eh Chineke! You this small small children. Ekuuse o, eyin daddy wa,' Jude ends and gives a mockery greetings.

'Gettat joor. Just paining you that you couldn't reach any of your wives, and no be me spoil your phone, Abi Na me? You are shouting about me chatting just one girl, but you, you can manage 15 girls at once, in fact,' John knelt down in front of Jude in mockery, 'daddy wa, pray for us.'

‘Keep quiet joor,’ Jude slightly pushes John’s head as John stands and relaxes back to his bed, ‘you know I need to keep communication and good relationships with everyone because of ...’

‘Blah blah… keep the story for the gods,’ John cuts in and Jude smacks his head. He does same to Jude and they start their cat and rat fight.

About an hour after…

Jude and John arrive a little late for the rally. They stop their bike at the gate of the church and join the other teenagers with few adults that are on their way out of the church for the rally.

Jude, when he notices the people have seen him, he smiles charmingly and opens his arms wide, moving closer to them. Some boys retract that they may walk with him, he hugs some guys and most girls blush and wave at him as he winks at them, calling some gorgeous. He’s more like the people’s guy, loves the attention.

John angrily and reluctantly pays the bike man, who zooms off immediately. John joins the group too, he doesn't roll with everyone like his brother but he gets a lot of attention because his look is like his brother's and most people take him for Jude. He smiles at few, waves to some and when he sees Rose finally, he smiles widely and waves at her.

Rose could not reply immediately because she was leading the songs for the rally. After she ends the second song, she informs Titi that she wants to greet someone and that she should keep leading the songs. Titi could not be any happier.

'Hey,' John greets.

'Hi, John,' she answers shyly, putting her hair curves behind her ears. She wears an off-shoulder top with a high waist flare shirt and she ties a chiffon scarf on her head which leaves her hair curves in front.

'Your cloth is beautiful,' John compliments.

She blushes, 'you look cute too.'

John has a white t-shirt and an Adire shirt over it. He has black jeans on, slightly ripped at it ankle.

'Yeah, thank you. How has been your day?' John asks.

'Well, it has been quite chatty,' she gives him a knowing look.

Almost an hour after…

'Àbọ̀ ré o Jésù

Ati jí ṣẹ́ to rán wa

Àbọ̀ ré o Jésù...' the rally group sing whilst returning into the church auditorium.

They all move into the church and drop the drums and other things they took along for the rally.

John and Rose are left in the church for others have left to join the people on the crusade ground.

'So, hmm...what would you be doing this weekend?' asks John

'Nothing much, just some cleaning and ...' the bell rings, signifying the crusade has started which interrupts Rose. The sound alerts both Rose and John and they immediately knew they've overstayed. They exchange smiles and walk to the crusade ground taking different routes.

At the operation site…

Then, with a loud siren that fills that street makes the gang alerted and shocked and worried and... everything.

‘Shit! Move it,’ Josh yells

Stella tries to hasten the guys through the walkie-talkie they have on but when she realizes she would be the first to get caught, she drives the car away, farther away from their operation site. *Na who wan die?* She thinks.

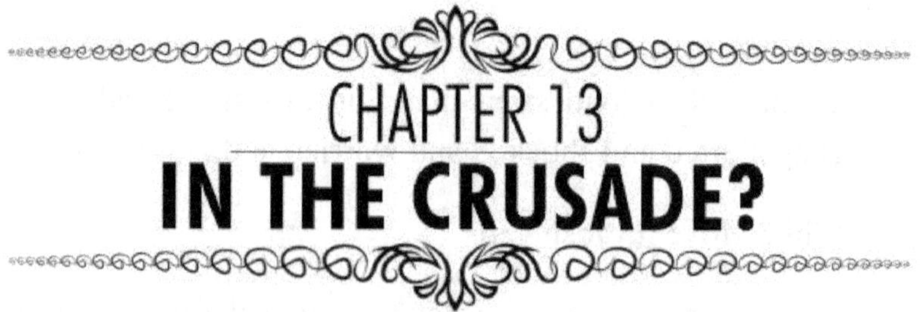

CHAPTER 13: IN THE CRUSADE?

Ralph throws the bag to the person at the left of the compound which is Moyo as planned but in a hurry this time because everyone has to run for their lives.

Moyo is calm and collected, like the boss with absolute control.

'You all take me for a fool, let's see who the fool is now,' she had said to herself during the course of the planning against robbing the politician's house.

Moyo, as nominated to spy on the house, has taken note of all the entrances and exits in the mansion, the number of guards, the number of rooms and other sorts. She, during the spy, notes a secret door she discovers that leads out of the mansion to a different street. As she joins the gang planning, she has hers going on too.

She carries the huge bag and rolls it out through the secret door.

'Sorry brothers, but you have to battle with the police now,' she gives a wicked giggle and exits the compound.

Shortly after…

Cynthia stumbles on the flowers by the fence built around the mansion. She struggles to stand and takes off her facemask.

'Stupid facemask,' she says.

Then she realizes a policeman is nearby.

'Hey!' he yells.

She hurries from the flower and stands straight like she never struggled and begins to run, she's light, just like light, runs with speed and leaves the policemen behind.

She couldn't run for long, more like a cheetah, her energy is dropping but she keeps going, for she isn't the predator here but the pry. She runs further a little bit more and starts to hear voices of a multitude that sounds like a roaring sea.

With reflex action, she turns in the direction of the voices and when she finally sees where the voices are from, she sees heads, a sea of heads.

Without thinking much, she rushes into the multitude and gets mingled. She looks around her, trying to see if she can find any trace of the police and when she could not find any, she lowers herself and her butts hit something. She jerks forward.

‘Oh! It's a chair,’ she exclaims, sits and relaxes completely on it.

She exhales deeply and closes her eyes.

‘How the fuck did you get here, Cynthia? You’ve always been an idiot, no shock, but...’ she says as she takes off her gloves and places it aside.

She bows her head and signs.

She suddenly felt at ease, calm and collected. Her mind becomes peaceful and she starts to take in her environment. Strange, though she is used to partying with crowds choking themselves but it had never made her feel this way before. She feels at home, she has forgotten the reason she is there a few minutes ago. That feeling is rear. She hasn’t felt anything close to it in years.

Few words reach her inner ears and it starts forming meaning for her. It must have been from the preacher.

'The devil, the thief, who is to kill, steal and destroy may have used the worldly things like cars, small money that would seem so big, and damnation that he wraps with pleasure wrapper to take the perfect peace from you then you will get bothered with anything that you do but that is why the Holy Spirit has directed your path here this evening to find the perfect peace, the true peace in Christ. Only Jesus can save. If you are here and you...' the evangelist makes an altar call.

Like a real voice, she hears 'stand' and she stands. Not knowing how but not discomforting, her feet move as if they have their minds and they are not telling her what they want but she feels at ease about it all.

Before she knows it, she's already in front where the evangelist has ordered those that want to accept Jesus, the giver of the perfect gift.

'Thank you, Jesus. So, I want you all to say after me. Say, father...' the evangelist orders.

And the people repeat and so does Cynthia but as she repeats, the things she has done flash through her mind with a speed of light. The day she killed an old man to get his belongings; the day she disturbed the peace of a small family and took their possessions; how she caused a fire outbreak in a few apartments to erase tracks and so many other things. She has been a bitterness toward this world and has caused people pain. She wonders what she has done to deserve this peace she feels.

After the confession and prayers, the evangelist directs them to the counselors around who are to take their names, phone numbers, and home addresses for follow-up.

A counselor has called Cynthia aside, slightly from the crusade ground and as her details are been collected, she sees a police officer looking up and down, obviously for someone.

Cynthia moves away from the counselor to the policeman who is wondering. She taps him and stretches her arms forward, folded.

The policeman looks agape, 'what on earth… just happened?' he mutters to himself then he suddenly snaps out of it, hardens his face and takes a handcuff from his pocket, and uses it on Cynthia's hands. He leads her to their waiting vehicle as he speaks into the walkie-talkie he has on.

THE BEGINNING.

www.ingramcontent.com/pod-product-compliance
Lightning Source LLC
LaVergne TN
LVHW052049160826
845678LV00015B/3140

* 9 7 9 8 8 4 9 7 6 0 1 2 4 *